VIKING KESTREL
Viking Penguin Inc., 40 West 23rd Street
New York, New York 10010, U.S.A.
Penguin Books Canada Limited, 2801 John Street
Markham, Ontario, Canada L3R 1B4
Text copyright © Karen Erickson, 1987
Illustrations copyright © Maureen Roffey, 1987
All rights reserved
First published in 1987 by Viking Penguin Inc.
Published simultaneously in Canada
Set in Sabon.
Printed in Italy by L.E.G.O.
Produced for the publishers by
Sadie Fields Productions Ltd, London.

1   2   3   4   5   91   90   89   88   87

It's Dark – But I'm Not Scared

Karen Erickson and Maureen Roffey

Viking Kestrel

It is so dark – everywhere.
I can't see a thing.

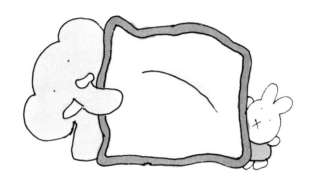

I wonder what's here,
or there,
or anywhere. It's scarey.

But wait.
I'm not really scared.
I can be brave at night.

My room is the same.
Only the lights are out.

My window is there.
Only the shade is down.

My walls are the old daytime ones.

Even the floor is the same.
Those shapes are my toys in the corner.

I know my room is safe.
I know everything that is in it.

Darkness makes everything look
different, but it's really just the same.

Darkness makes everything look
different, but it's really just the same.

Night is a soft blanket that covers
my room and lets it sleep.

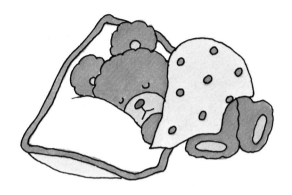

My room and I are comfortable
and cozy.

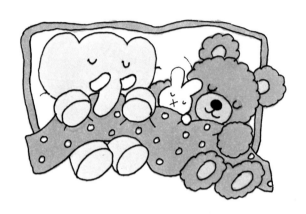

Look. I can be brave at night.

I can do it.

I did it.